D1194953

BAILEY

A Magic School for Girls Chapter Book

A.M. Luzzader

Illustrated by Anna Hilton

Published by Knowledge Forest Press
P.O. Box 6331
Logan, UT 84341

Ebook ISBN-13: 978-1-949078-33-6
Paperback ISBN-13: 978-1-949078-34-3

Cover design by Sleepy Fox Studio

Editing by Chadd VanZanten

Interior illustrations by Anna Hilton

CONTENTS

CHAPTER 1
EIGHT IS GREAT

Bailey Jones couldn't wait for her eighth birthday. Eight years old was the age when a girl could begin going to magic school.

"Eight is the perfect age to learn magic," said Miss Annie.

You may already know that Miss Annie was the director of Annette McGill's School of Magic for Magically Gifted Girls, which was also known as Miss Annie's Magic School. Miss Annie was a tall and dignified witch. She was thin, with a long face, long nose, and beautiful long hair that was as white as snow. She wore a black, close-fitting witch's dress and a tall witch's hat that rose into the air like a black tower.

Miss Annie always said, "Girls who are younger than eight must concentrate on learning to read and solve math problems. They must learn the skills that are essential for using magic."

And that is what Bailey was trying hard to do. She read lots of books, studied every night, and always did her homework. Miss Annie's school was not for all girls, of course. It was only for those girls who believed in magic and wanted to learn about it.

"Girls older than eight begin to lose their belief in magic," said Miss Annie. "If girls get too old, they have trouble believing in magical and mysterious things, which makes it very hard to learn how to use magic."

Yes, eight was the perfect age to attend Miss Annie's Magic School, but Bailey always wished that she could have attended magic school even earlier.

For example, when Bailey was only five years old, she loved looking at the magic textbooks that her older sister, Kiara, brought home from Miss Annie's Magic School. Even though Bailey couldn't read yet, she flipped through the pages for hours, amazed by the puzzling words and mysterious pictures.

When she was six years old, Bailey and her two best friends, Julie and Kate, often pretended they were already in magic school. They took turns playing the part of Miss Annie, writing lessons on the playroom chalkboard and pretending to cast the most wondrous magical spells. They cast pretend spells to grow magical flowers. They cast pretend spells to water the flowers, and then pretended that magical rainbows appeared over the flowers.

Soon Bailey turned seven. That's when she began asking Kiara all about magic school.

"Is Miss Annie nice?" Bailey asked Kiara. "Is magical homework hard? What spells did you learn today?"

She watched Kiara practicing her magic and

casting spells, and when Kiara wasn't around, Bailey would even imitate Kiara, using a pencil for a magic wand and repeating the magic words as best she could remember.

Then, at last, Bailey turned eight!

That summer, before she was registered at Miss Annie's Magic School, Bailey read every magic book she could get her hands on. She read Kiara's magic school textbooks. She read magic books from the library. She read dusty old magic books and brand new magazines about magic. Reading was Bailey's favorite activity, and magic was her favorite thing to read about.

Bailey imagined all the things she would do after she learned magic. She might blow a bubblegum bubble and magically make it as big as a beachball.

5

She would clean her room using magic while she lay in her bed. And she could send her friends magical notes, which would arrive in their bedrooms on waves of magical sparkles.

Bailey just couldn't wait to start her classes at Annette McGill's School of Magic for Magically Gifted Girls.

Finally, the day arrived. It was Bailey's first day of magic school!

That morning, Bailey's mom knocked lightly on her bedroom door, then opened Bailey's door. But Bailey was already awake! She had even made her bed and brushed her teeth.

"I was coming to wake you up," said Bailey's mom, "but it looks like I didn't need to."

"I was too excited," said Bailey. "I hardly slept at all last night!"

"I'm glad you are excited," said Bailey's mom. "Get dressed and then come eat your breakfast."

Getting ready to go to Annette McGill's School of Magic for Magically Gifted Girls was different than getting ready for regular school. Uniforms were required for magic school. There was a crisp white shirt, a dark skirt or slacks, a necktie or bow, and special shoes. Bailey's friend Kate didn't like wearing the uniform.

"I'm an artist!" said Kate. "I like bright colors and unique jewelry!"

Bailey didn't mind wearing the uniform. She liked how the uniform looked. When she put it on, she looked like a student of Miss Annie's Magic School, and that is what Bailey liked most of all.

One reason the students were required to wear uniforms was that ordinary clothing might be spoiled at magic school. If you were making a magic potion and it splashed on an ordinary blouse or skirt, the potion would leave a nasty stain. The uniforms prevented such mishaps.

Bailey put on her pink glasses, and then pulled her hair into a high puff and smoothed the sides with hair gel. When she finished, she looked at herself in the mirror and smiled. At last, she not only *looked* like a magic school student, she *was* a magic school student!

Bailey added two pink barrettes to match her glasses. Pink was Bailey's favorite color. Even though she liked the school uniforms, she was glad that she could add a little color with her glasses and hair barrettes. She also had a pink backpack which she would use to carry her brand-new wand, textbooks, and lunch bag.

On most mornings, Bailey ate cereal for breakfast. However, when Bailey sat down at the kitchen table, she was surprised to see that her mom had prepared a special breakfast.

"Wow," said Bailey, "Bacon, eggs, toast, and, what's this? A smoothie?"

Bailey's mom smiled. "Yes, it's made from dragon's wort juice, which helps with magic ability. I thought it might be good for your first day."

"Thanks, mom," said Bailey. "You're the best!"

Bailey had waited for years to go to magic school. She had read about magic school, asked her big sister about magic school, and had even pretended to *be* in magic school. Bailey's first day of magic school had finally arrived, and she was sure that nothing could possibly go wrong.

Unfortunately, Bailey was mistaken.

CHAPTER 2

JULIE AND KATE

When it was almost time to leave for school, the door-bell rang. Bailey answered the door and saw her two best friends, Kate and Julie. Kate had short black hair and Julie had long blond hair. They were both eight years old, just like Bailey, and both were wearing their magic school uniforms.

"Your uniforms look awesome," said Bailey.

"Thanks," said Julie, straightening her skirt.

But Kate looked down at her skirt and said, "Oh, I don't know. This isn't what I usually wear." Kate usually wore very bright colors, lots of bracelets and necklaces, and shirts printed with cartoon characters. Bailey understood why Julie might not like the magic school uniform with its dark colors and plain design.

9

"But you look like you belong at Miss Annie's Magic School now," said Bailey. "And that's really good."

"You're really excited for school, aren't you Bailey?" asked Kate.

"Aren't you?" replied Bailey. "I hardly slept at all last night. I was just so excited. I've been waiting for this day for ages!"

Kate nodded. "Yeah, I think it will be fun."

Julie shrugged. "It's just more school. I guess it'll be okay. But I'd rather be home playing with Moonbeam."

Moonbeam was Julie's black cat.

"How is Moonbeam?" asked Bailey.

"She's so cute," said Julie. "I miss her so much while I'm at school."

Bailey's mom came to the door and had the girls pose on the porch for a first-day-of-school photo. Then the three friends walked the two blocks to Annette McGill's School of Magic for Magically Gifted Girls.

Bailey had a fluttery feeling in her stomach that felt a little uncomfortable, but she knew it was just because she couldn't wait to learn all about magic.

Her older sister, Kiara, was only three years older

than Bailey, and she was already flying on broomsticks, cooking up magic potions, and casting simple spells with her wand. Kiara could do the Fetch spell, which she used to bring her things, like a glass of water or a book from downstairs. There were also funny spells, like the Magic Bubble spell, which produced an endless supply of soap bubbles from the end of Kiara's wand.

Bailey had been to Miss Annie's Magic School before. She went there to see Kiara's magic recitals and performances. After Kiara's most recent recital, their mom spoke for a while with Miss Annie. Bailey listened closely as Miss Annie talked about magic.

"Anyone with a desire to learn magic can do so," Miss Annie had said. "It doesn't take any special abilities or talents. Just lots of hard work, study, and practice."

Bailey knew that there weren't many magic schools in the country, so she felt very lucky that she and her friends lived so close to one. She was going to do just what Miss Annie had said--work hard, study, and practice. Would that really be enough?

Annette McGill's School of Magic for Magically Gifted Girls was a large old mansion of red brick. The mansion was tall with many fancy windows, towers, and a weather vane with a bat on top. Vines with deep green leaves climbed the walls. Bailey thought it looked a little spooky, but also beautiful.

Bailey and her friends went inside and Bailey learned that she would be in Miss Betsy Bumble's class. Miss Betsy was short and round. It was the first time Bailey had a teacher who was shorter than she was! Miss Betsy's eyes

sparkled merrily. Her hair was silver and curled up into a twist. She wore a purple witch's hat with a wide, floppy brim. The witch's hat meant that Miss Betsy had graduated from magic university.

"Are you ready for some magic?" Miss Betsy asked Bailey when she entered the classroom.

Bailey grinned and nodded. She knew already that she would like Miss Betsy a lot. Julie was in the same class. Kate was in Mr. Jack Jasper's class down the hall.

Julie and Bailey found their desks close to each

other. They sat down and grabbed the notebooks, pens, and beginner's wands from their backpacks, then arranged them on their desks.

When the bell rang for class to start, Miss Betsy walked to the front of the room. With a twinkle in her eyes, she raised her arms into the air. In one hand she held a magic wand. It was twisted and braided, like a length of grapevine. For a moment, she only stood smiling and watching her new students. The students looked back at Miss Betsy, wondering what would happen next.

After another moment, Miss Betsy shouted, "Party-fah-loo-la!" and waved her wand in the air.

Glitter and balloons suddenly fell from the ceiling. Bright, happy music played. Then, the desks and chairs rose into the air and danced around the classroom, all while the students were still sitting in them!

Bailey laughed as the music played and the balloons bounced around the room. "I love magic!"

But when she looked over at Julie, she saw that her friend seemed nervous, and was holding tightly onto her desk.

"I don't like being up so high!" Julie yelled.

After a while, the music grew quieter, and the desks and chairs returned to their places on the floor.

Even though there had been glitter, confetti, and balloons all over the room just minutes before, it all vanished and the room was sparkling clean again.

"Wasn't that fun?" asked Miss Betsy.

Almost everyone, except Julie, nodded in agreement.

"Magic can be lots of fun," said Miss Betsy, "but before you can throw a party-fah-loo-la and other big spells, you must learn the basics."

Bailey leaned forward in her chair. She wanted to learn everything about magic, even the boring basics.

"For example," said Miss Betsy, "you must learn the difference between a potion and an elixir."

Bailey raised her hand high into the air and waved it.

Miss Betsy pointed to Bailey and said, "Yes? Do you have a question my dear?"

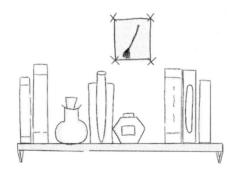

"No, ma'am," said Bailey, "but I do know the difference between potions and elixirs. A potion has various ingredients, such as snail slime or mandrake. An elixir is made from water mixed with magical energy like moonlight or tree dreams. There are also magical concoctions, which is when you take an ordinary liquid, like orange juice or chocolate milk, and make it into a magic liquid."

"By the itching of my thumbs!" declared Miss Betsy, her eyes wide. "That's correct. What is your name, young witch?"

"Bailey Jones, ma'am."

"And how do you know so much about potions and elixirs?" asked Miss Betsy.

"This past summer I read a book from the library all about potions, elixirs, and concoctions," Bailey answered.

Just then, Bailey heard what sounded like someone laughing. It was as though one of the students behind her was laughing at what she said. But all Bailey had said was that she'd read a book, so she ignored it.

"I'm impressed!" said Miss Betsy. The brim of her witch's hat wobbled as she nodded. "You see, students? The basics may not be very exciting, but if you're dedicated like Bailey, they're not so bad. And once you master the basics, you'll be able to cast spells that are more useful and more fun. At the end of the term, if you work hard, we can throw an even bigger party-fah-loo-la."

Julie raised her hand. "Do the chairs and desks have to dance and fly up into the air? I'd rather stay close to the ground."

Miss Betsy smiled. "Yes, if you prefer your chair on the ground, that is perfectly fine. There's more than one way to enjoy a party. But I must warn you, part of your schooling here at Miss Annie's Magic School will involve flying on broomsticks."

Julie didn't seem very pleased with this answer, but we shall leave that matter for another time.

The rest of the school day passed quickly. Miss Betsy explained the school rules and classroom regulations. She gave the students a tour of the academy. There were a lot of safety rules that the students had to remember.

"As first-year magic students," said Miss Betsy, "you mustn't cast certain spells without an adult wizard or witch nearby."

"What spells are those?" asked Bailey.

"I'll give you a full list," said Miss Betsy, "but one kind of spell that requires adult supervision, for example, is spells that start fires."

There were other rules, too. Students were not allowed in the school's basement or on its roof. And they could only drink magic potions if they had permission from a teacher.

"Most of all," Miss Betsy warned, "you must be careful to always pay attention to instructions and follow them carefully. Magic can be fun and useful, but if you are careless, accidents can happen, and I don't want any of you dear students to get hurt. That wouldn't be good at all."

Bailey could tell that Miss Betsy really loved her students and loved teaching. Her first day of magic school had been just what she imagined it would be like. It was exciting, interesting and fun.

However, little did Bailey know that she would soon understand why safety rules were so important at Annette McGill's School of Magic for Magically Gifted Girls.

CHAPTER 4

THE BASICS OF MAGIC

At the end of the first day, Miss Betsy addressed the class. "There will be no homework tonight," she announced. "There will be plenty of homework later, but for tonight you may rest and relax."

The students seemed glad about this. They whispered happily to each other. Bailey, on the other hand, was slightly disappointed. She was ready to start learning about magic!

"However," added Miss Bailey, her eyes twinkling, "if you have time and you want a little work to do, you may read the first ten pages of our textbook."

Bailey looked at her brand-new text book. It was called *A Beginner's Guide to Magic: Everything You*

Need to Know to Cast Basic Magical Spells without Turning Yourself into a Frog (725th Edition).

That evening, Bailey read the first ten pages of the textbook. She found it very interesting, so she read the next ten pages. These were quite interesting, too, so Bailey read a few chapters.

Then, she took a flashlight into bed with her so she could read a few more pages before falling asleep, and to her surprise she soon finished the entire book! Bailey had read the entire class textbook on her first day of school! And she loved every page!

Bailey thought that now that she had read the

book that she might really be able to cast some of the spells she'd seen her sister Kiara cast. But then Bailey remembered what Miss Betsy said about studying carefully and following directions, so she decided to wait for more instruction from her teacher.

The next day in class, Miss Betsy asked if anyone had read the first ten pages. Bailey raised her hand into the air, and she waited for Miss Betsy to call on her.

"Yes, Bailey?" said Miss Betsy with a smile. "Were you able to read the first ten pages?"

"Yes!" Bailey replied. "And then I read the rest of the book!"

Miss Betsy raised her eyebrows. "Very good, Bailey!" she cried.

Bailey smiled. She wanted to do very well in magic school, and she hoped Miss Betsy would be proud of her. However, once again Bailey thought she heard somebody laugh. It was someone behind her. She swiveled around in her seat to look, but she didn't see anyone laughing, and Miss Betsy was speaking, so Bailey turned back to the front to listen.

The magic lessons finally began! Miss Betsy taught the class some basic concepts of magic.

"Most witches and warlocks use a magic item to

cast spells," explained Miss Betsy. "The most common magic item is a wand."

Miss Betsy held up her wand for the class to see. It looked very powerful and quite old. It had grapevine branches that twisted around each other in a very pretty pattern.

"Wands are easy to create, and they are easy to use and carry," Miss Betsy continued. "You use them the same way you use a paint brush or pencil. Just point your wand where you want the magic to go."

The students picked up their beginner's wands and pointed them here and there.

Miss Betsy said, "We've supplied you with these beginner's wands so that you can practice basic magic, but soon you'll make your own magic item. Does anyone know what other kinds of things you can use to cast spells?"

A few of the other girls raised their hands, but Bailey's hand was in the air first.

Miss Betsy pointed at Bailey and said, "Yes, Bailey?"

Bailey sat up straight and recited what she'd read in the class textbook. "Some witches and warlocks use magic rings, staffs, crystals, and even ordinary household items like spoons and umbrellas."

This time, Bailey was sure that someone behind her chuckled. Or maybe it was a scoff. Whatever it was, it wasn't nice. Bailey was about to turn around again to see, but Miss Betsy continued.

"Very good, Bailey," she said. "Students, did you hear that? Staffs, crystals, and just about anything you can easily carry can be used to cast your spells."

The rest of the morning was much the same. Miss Betsy would ask a question, and Bailey would sit up tall and raise her hand. Miss Betsy didn't call on Bailey every time, but Bailey knew all of the answers to the questions Miss Betsy asked. And, oddly, each time Bailey answered a question, she heard someone behind her scoff or laugh.

When it was time for recess, the other girls rushed outside, but Bailey went to Miss Betsy's desk.

"I really enjoyed reading the textbook," said Bailey. "Especially the parts about proper wand position and the basic ingredients for light spells."

"My stars," said Miss Betsy. "I'm so pleased you're enjoying class. I don't think I've ever known a student who read the entire book on the very first day."

Bailey shrugged. "When you find something interesting, it's fun to learn more."

Miss Betsy's twinkly eyes scrunched up as she grinned. "I think you'll do very well here at Miss Annie's Magic School, my dear."

Bailey said, "I was wondering if you had some extra books on magic that I could borrow. I'll be very careful with them and will be sure to return them."

"Of course!" said Miss Betsy. "I'm glad you asked." Miss Betsy went to her bookcase. She put her finger on her chin as she looked at her books. Then she pulled three books. "One on flying, one on cooking spells, and one on unicorns." She handed them to Bailey.

"Unicorns?" asked Bailey. "They're real?"

"Of course they're real!" said Miss Betsy. "Unicorns, dragons, and fairies are all real. You might not see them as much anymore, but they do exist."

"Wow, that's so cool," said Bailey. "Thank you so much for the books. I'll try to read the books this weekend and get them back to you by Monday."

"No rush, my dear," said Miss Betsy. "Just enjoy them."

"Oh, I will," said Bailey.

Bailey went back to her desk. After she'd placed the books into her backpack, she noticed one of her classmates, a girl named Rebecca, standing by the classroom door. Bailey thought that Rebecca's desk was somewhere behind her own. Rebecca seemed to be watching Bailey. When their eyes met, Rebecca frowned, and then she left the classroom.

CHAPTER 5

STRESS AT RECESS

Bailey went outside to join the rest of the class at recess. She saw girls sitting in the grass weaving baskets for their wands. She saw other girls playing a game of Witchy, May I. Then she saw her best friends, Kate and Julie. It looked like they were playing hopscotch, which aside from magic, was one of Bailey's favorite things to play.

Bailey walked toward her friends and the hopscotch grid they'd drawn on the ground, but suddenly Rebecca approached her. She was with several other girls, and they all stood in front of Bailey, blocking her way.

"You think you're really smart, don't you?" asked Rebecca.

"Huh?" was all Bailey could say.

"It's only the second day of school, and you're already trying to be the teacher's pet," said Rebecca. The other girls nodded and agreed.

"The teacher's what?" said Bailey, wrinkling her nose. She'd never heard that before.

"You're trying to be the teacher's pet," repeated Rebecca. "You're trying to be Miss Betsy's favorite. You're trying to make the rest of us look lazy and stupid."

"No, I'm not!" cried Bailey.

"Then why do you have to answer every single question?" Rebecca demanded. "Why do you have to act like a know-it-all?"

"I'm not a teacher's pet," said Bailey. "I'm not a know-it-all. I just love magic and magic school and magic lessons!"

Rebecca turned to one of the other girls. Her name was Mary. "It's so annoying when the same person always answers all the questions, right Mary?"

"Definitely," said Mary. "No one likes a show-off!"

The other girls joined in. "Big-mouth!" they shouted as they walked away. "Know-it-all! Teacher's pet! Show-off!"

Bailey's cheeks grew hot, and she felt as though she might cry. Why had those girls said such unkind things? Bailey didn't feel like playing hopscotch with Kate and Julie anymore. However, Kate and Julie must have spotted Bailey, because they waved at Bailey and came over to her.

"Is everything okay, Bailey?" Julie asked. "You look upset."

Bailey looked across the playground and spotted Rebecca, who was still watching her.

"Everything's fine," said Bailey, even though she really did feel upset.

"Are you sure?" said Kate. "You seem sad. Is it because Miss Annie's school is hard? I've been having trouble with the potions in my class. They all have icky ingredients and I don't want to drink them."

"I'd rather not talk about school," said Bailey.

"That's okay," said Julie. "Let's go play."

They went back to the hopscotch grid. Bailey tried to have fun, but she couldn't help thinking about what Rebecca and her friends had said. She was glad when recess ended.

CHAPTER 6
NOT THE TEACHER'S PET

When they returned from recess, Miss Betsy told the class that she had some really important lessons that she needed to teach them.

"I'm sure you have all practiced fire drills at your other schools," said Miss Betsy. "Fire drills are very important and can save lives. Here at Miss Annie's Magic School we will also practice fire drills. But today I want to talk to you about magical fire. It's different from regular fire. You can't put it out with water or a blanket or even a fire extinguisher. Luckily, there is a simple spell that you can cast that will put it out."

Miss Betsy was writing *Retire Dire Fire* on the whiteboard. "Does anyone know anything about this spell?" she asked as she wrote.

Bailey knew about that spell, and her hand went straight up into the air. Of course Bailey knew the answer. She'd read about it in the textbook the night before. She stretched out her arm and waggled her hand to get Miss Betsy's attention.

Then, behind her, Bailey heard Rebecca whisper, "Teacher's pet!" Rebecca said it quietly, so that only Bailey heard it. She hissed again: "Show-off!"

Bailey blushed and quickly put her hand down.

Miss Betsy finished writing on the board and turned back around. "Does anyone know it?"

No one else raised a hand.

"What about you, Bailey?" Miss Betsy asked. "Do you know the spell?"

Bailey didn't like the other girls making fun of her, so even though she'd read about the spell to put out fires, she shook her head no.

"Oh," said Miss Betsy in surprise. "Well, that's okay. I'll teach it to you all right now."

Miss Betsy taught the whole class the spell and told them to always remember it because it was so important for safety. To put out a magical fire, a witch needed only to spin around three times, tap the tip of her nose, point her wand, and say, "Goodbye flames, goodbye smoke. Retire dire fire, and that's no joke."

"You never know when there might be an emergency and you'll need this spell," said Miss Betsy. In the middle of the classroom she lit a magical fire whose flames flickered without burning the floor or anything else in the classroom. Then she called on a few students to come to the front of the class to demonstrate their newly learned magical ability, but Bailey did not raise her hand or volunteer. She just stayed at her desk.

CHAPTER 7

SAD WEEKEND

There was no school the next day because it was the weekend. Even though Bailey had enjoyed learning about magic for most of the week, she was glad to have some time at home. She didn't want to be around Rebecca or her friends.

Bailey thought many times about reading the books she borrowed from Miss Betsy, but each time she opened one of the books, she remembered Rebecca and her friends laughing at her and taunting her. Bailey thought of the cruel names they called her. "Teacher's pet." "Big mouth." This made her feel sad, and she put the books back in her backpack, where they stayed all weekend.

Bailey didn't read any of her magic class textbook,

either. She tried to find things to do that didn't involve magic, but the truth was, there wasn't anything she liked more than magic. And so Bailey missed reading about great witches and wizards. She wanted to practice the spells her class had been learning. And she wanted to talk more about magic with her sister Kiara. But all these things just made her remember how bad she had felt when Rebecca and her friends had stopped her.

So Bailey didn't do anything magic related the entire weekend. It was a boring and sad weekend, and it seemed to last forever. She was glad when it was Monday and time for magic school again, but she had decided that she wouldn't volunteer in class anymore, and she wouldn't answer questions. Bailey decided to just learn the lessons privately and keep quiet, even though she knew she wouldn't learn as much or as quickly.

When she walked into class on Monday, Miss Betsy saw her and said, "Oh, Bailey! Did you read all of those books?"

"No, ma'am," said Bailey.

"Ah, yes," replied Miss Betsy. "There were too many to read in one weekend. Which ones did you read?"

"I didn't read any of them, Miss Betsy," said Bailey.

"Didn't you like them?" asked Miss Betsy with a frown.

Bailey shrugged. "I don't know. I didn't start them. Do you want them back?"

Miss Betsy had a concerned look on her face. "No, that's okay. Keep them as long as you need. I just thought you would have started them by now."

CHAPTER 8
NO GOOD ANSWERS

In the weeks that followed, Bailey didn't volunteer to help with any projects or demonstrations, and she didn't raise her hand when Miss Betsy asked questions, even though she almost always knew the right answer.

When Miss Betsy asked, "Who can tell me how many eggs dragons usually lay at one time?"

Bailey thought, "Three." But she did not raise her hand, even though that was the correct answer.

When Miss Betsy asked, "What color is the flame of the Everlasting Torch spell?"

Bailey whispered, "Purple." But still she did not raise her hand.

MISS BETSY

Miss Betsy asked, "Who can recite the spell for the Perfect Marshmallow Roasting Flame?" Bailey sat on her hands and pressed her lips together. She wanted so badly to raise her hand and tell Miss Betsy that she not only knew the answer, but she could cast the spell.

But she especially didn't want Rebecca or her friends to call her a teacher's pet or something worse or to laugh at her again. So week after week, Bailey stayed quiet and didn't answer any of the teacher's questions during the lessons.

One day at the end of school, Miss Betsy asked Bailey to stay and talk to her after class.

"I was just wondering," said Miss Betsy, "If you finished reading those books you borrowed."

"Yes, I did," said Bailey. She pulled them out of her bookbag and gave them back to Miss Betsy.

"Did you enjoy them?" asked Miss Betsy.

Bailey looked to see if any of her classmates were still in the room and listening, but no one else was there. "I enjoyed them very much. Thank you."

"Would you like to borrow some more?" Miss Betsy asked.

As a matter of fact, Bailey did want to borrow more. She almost said yes, but then she thought about what Rebecca would say if she found out. She shook her head no.

"Let me know if you change your mind," said Miss Betsy.

"I will," said Bailey. She turned to leave.

"Just a minute," said Miss Betsy. "There's something else I wanted to talk to you about."

"What is it?" asked Bailey.

"I've been looking over your assignments and test scores," said Miss Betsy. "Your grades are almost perfect. You always complete your homework on time. You're at the top of the class."

Bailey was glad to hear this, but she tried to not look too excited.

"But you never raise your hand in class anymore," Miss Betsy continued. "It would be good for you and the other students if you participated more."

"Umm," said Bailey. How could she explain why she wasn't volunteering to help or answer questions anymore? Rebecca and her friends hadn't been teasing her lately, but would that change if she started answering questions again?

"Just think about it," said Miss Betsy. "You're a smart girl, and you're going to make an excellent witch. But everyone learns best when they share what they know."

"Okay," said Bailey, but she had no plans to change how she acted in class. No one needed to know how much she knew about magic.

CHAPTER 9
BLAZING MARSHMALLOWS

Miss Betsy wanted the entire class to learn the Perfect Marshmallow Roasting Flame spell before autumn break so that they could all roast perfect marshmallows with their families. The spell created a magical flame that was warm enough to make the marshmallows brown on the outside and gooey on the inside, but it wasn't hot enough to burn them black or melt them off the stick. With the Perfect Marshmallow Roasting Flame spell, everyone got a perfect marshmallow every time.

And so Miss Betsy led the students outside to the school's playground and arranged them into a circle. Then she gave them each a marshmallow roasting stick and a marshmallow to go on the end.

"Who wants to go first?" asked Miss Betsy with a smile.

But it seemed the class was having a hard time remembering the spell. Bailey knew the spell, of course. There was almost nothing Miss Betsy had taught that Bailey didn't know. But she couldn't let anyone know. She didn't want to be the teacher's pet.

Bailey's friend Julie finally raised her hand. "I'll give it a try," she said.

Julie had often seemed distracted and bored in magic class, so Bailey was surprised to see her volunteer.

Bailey didn't think of Julie as trying to be a know-it-all or a teacher's pet. In fact, at the moment, Julie seemed quite brave.

Julie brushed her blonde hair over her shoulders and walked into the circle of students. She turned in a circle, but she turned the wrong way, then she pointed her wand at the ground and said, "Fire braze, no, that's not right, fire bright?"

"That's close, dear," said Miss Betsy. "Think about it and try again."

Just then a magical note for Miss Betsy arrived on a wave of magical sparks. The teacher snatched it out of the air and read it silently to herself.

"It seems I'm needed in the front office," said Miss Betsy. "Talk amongst yourselves, and I'll be right back. And don't eat your marshmallows!"

After Miss Betsy left, the other students began chatting with each other. Bailey watched as Julie whispered to herself and closed her eyes and bit her lip. She was trying to remember the spell.

Bailey walked up to her. "The way you cast the Perfect Marshmallow Roasting Flame spell is turn in a circle--to the right, not the left--and then say, 'Fire blaze, fire bright, make some flames for a gooey delight'."

"You know the spell?" Julie asked. "Why didn't you volunteer?"

Bailey shrugged. "No one likes a know-it-all."

"What are you talking about?" Julie said. "Are you embarrassed about what Rebecca and those other mean girls said about you?"

Bailey looked down and nodded.

"Is that why you've been so quiet in class? Never answering Miss Betsy's questions? Never volunteering to demonstrate the spells?" Julie asked.

Bailey nodded again and tried not to cry.

"You should ignore those girls," said Julie. "They're just jealous and mean. Everyone knows you're super smart, Bailey. You always teach me and Kate so much! Be yourself and ignore Rebecca."

"Maybe you're right," said Bailey.

"Thanks for helping me with the marshmallow spell," said Julie. "I think I've got it now."

Bailey thought about Rebecca and the other mean girls. Why was she embarrassed about what they said? Why did she care if they called her a teacher's pet? While Bailey thought about this, she didn't notice that Julie had turned in a circle to the right and waved her wand.

"Fire blaze, fire bright," said Julie, "make some wild flames tonight--um--oh, no! That's not right!"

That got Bailey's attention. "Wait!" she said to

Julie. "Wait for Miss Betsy!"

But it was too late. Julie had only meant to rehearse the spell, but the magical words had been spoken. A flame appeared on the grass of the playground. However, this was not a warm, harmless flame used to make marshmallows nice and gooey. This fire was bright and hot and it immediately began to spread fast!

"It's burning the grass!" Julie shouted. "It's burning the trees!"

Julie and Bailey stumbled back from the hot, dangerous flames. The other students screamed, threw down their marshmallow sticks, and began to run in all directions.

"Why is it burning out of control?" cried Julie.

"Because this isn't the marshmallow magic spell," said Bailey. "You've made some other magical fire!"

Julie said, "We need a fire extinguisher!"

"No, that won't help!" shouted Bailey.

"Turn on the sprinklers!" someone yelled.

"That won't help!" repeated Bailey.

"Call 9-1-1!" yelled someone else.

"Calm down, everyone!" cried Bailey. "You all should know that magic fire doesn't behave the same as a regular fire!"

54

"Oh, you're right!" moaned Julie, running her fingers through her hair. "But I can't remember how to put out a magical fire! What do I do? Tap the top of my head? Do a somersault?"

Most of the other students had run away. Smoke was rising over the playground. No one knew what to do.

No one, that is, except Bailey.

"Someone do something!" screamed Rebecca. "The whole school's going to burn down!"

But Bailey had already stepped forward and spun around three times. Next, she tapped the tip of her nose, pointed her wand, and said, "Goodbye flames, goodbye smoke. Retire dire fire, and that's no joke."

The fire and smoke vanished at once.

"Holy toadflax!" cried Miss Betsy when she returned to the playground. "I see someone accidentally learned the Wildfire spell."

"It was me," said Julie, bashfully raising her hand.

"Whew!" said Miss Betsy. "Well, at least you remembered the Retire Dire Fire spell so that you could put it out!"

"No, ma'am," said Julie in a quiet voice. "It was Bailey. She reminded me how to cast the Perfect Marshmallow Roasting Flame spell, but then I did it wrong, so then she put out the fire before it spread too much."

"Well done, Bailey," said Miss Betsy, looking up at Bailey and clapping her hands. "You've saved the day."

To Bailey's surprise, her classmates started clapping, too. Even Rebecca.

CHAPTER 10

PARTY TIME

On the last day of school before autumn break, Bailey sat in the front row of Miss Betsy's magic class.

When Miss Betsy asked what the name was of the wizard who invented the Jumping Slime potion, Bailey raised her hand and answered, "Walford E. Wimple."

When Miss Betsy asked what the most important ingredient in Energy Raising Shampoo was, Bailey raised her hand and answered, "Clovers."

And when Miss Betsy asked how to extinguish magical flames, Bailey raised her hand, but Miss Betsy called on Julie.

Julie sat up straight and said, "Spin three times, tap your nose, point your wand, and say, 'Goodbye flames, goodbye smoke. Retire dire fire, and that's no joke'."

"Very good, Julie!" said Miss Betsy.

When they went to recess, Bailey and her best friends, Julie and Kate, began to play hopscotch. Soon Rebecca and her friends walked up.

"So, you really are the teacher's pet," sneered Rebecca.

Julie and Kate watched Bailey to see how she'd answer. Bailey picked up her hopscotch marker and tossed it on the sidewalk. Then she hopped perfectly through the hopscotch grid, spun around, and looked at Rebecca.

"I guess I am the teacher's pet," said Bailey with a shrug.

Julie and Kate looked at Rebecca and her friends and said, "Yeah, she's the teacher's pet, and she's our friend."

Rebecca's teasing no longer bothered Bailey. She didn't care if Rebecca thought she was a know-it-all or a teacher's pet. Bailey loved magic, and she loved learning. She wasn't going to let anyone get in the way of that.

After recess, Miss Betsy told the class that they had done so well learning the beginning magic spells and following the rules that the class had earned a party.

"Bailey, will you do the honors?" Miss Betsy asked.

Bailey smiled. "Absolutely," she said. She walked to the front of the class. "Um, Julie," she said. "You might want to get off your chair."

"Thanks, Bailey," said Julie with a laugh.

Bailey waited for Julie to stand up, and then she said the magical words. "Party-fah-loo-la!"

Music played. Balloons, confetti, and glitter rained down on the students. Ice cream, delicious fruit, and other treats appeared all around the classroom. Once again, the chairs and desks floated and danced around the classroom. Everyone laughed and enjoyed the party, especially Bailey and her friend Julie.

After school, Julie and Bailey waited outside for their friend Kate so they could all walk home together.

"That was a fun party. I love dancing," said Julie, "on the ground!"

Bailey laughed.

"You know, Bailey," said Julie, "I'm really pleased."

"About the party?" asked Bailey. "I am, too!"

"No," said Julie. "I mean that I'm glad you've decided to be yourself again. I'm glad you can ignore what those mean girls say. But, yes, you sure know how to throw a good party."

"Well, we have a great teacher," said Bailey looking across the playground at Miss Betsy, who was directing the bus lines.

Miss Betsy caught sight of Bailey and Julie. She waved at the girls and they smiled and waved back.

"You were right, Julie," said Bailey. "I shouldn't care if a mean girl thinks I'm the teacher's pet. And as long as I'm a student here at Annette McGill's School of Magic for Magically Gifted Girls, I never will."

PLEASE LEAVE A REVIEW

Thank you for reading this book. We hope you enjoyed it! We would really appreciate it if you would please take a moment to review *Bailey: A Magic School for Girls Chapter Book* on Amazon or other retail sites. Thank you!

WWW.AMLUZZADER.COM

- blog
- freebies
- newsletter
- contact info

OTHER BOOKS BY
A.M. Luzzader

A Magic School for Girls Chapter Book

For ages 6-8

OTHER BOOKS BY
A.M. Luzzader

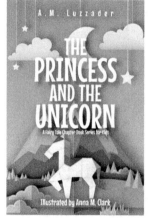

A Fairy Tale Chapter Book Series for Kids

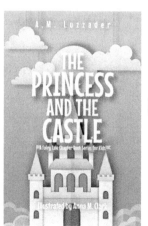

For ages
6-8

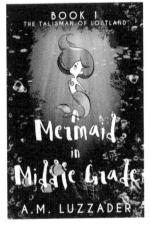

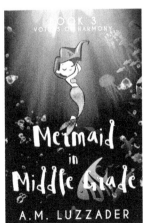

OTHER BOOKS BY
A.M. Luzzader

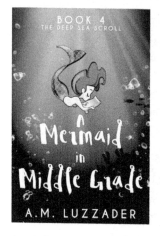 

A Mermaid in Middle Grade
Books 4–6

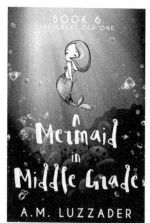

For ages
8-12

OTHER BOOKS BY
A.M. Luzzader

Hannah Saves the World
Books 1-3

For ages
8-12

ABOUT THE AUTHOR

A.M. Luzzader is an award-winning children's author who writes chapter books and middle grade books. She specializes in writing books for preteens. A.M.'s fantasy adventure series 'A Mermaid in Middle Grade' is a magical coming of age book series for ages 8-12. She is also the author of the 'Hannah Saves the

World' series, which is a children's mystery adventure, also for ages 8-12.

A.M. decided she wanted to write fun stories for kids when she was still a kid herself. By the time she was in fourth grade, she was already writing short stories. In fifth grade, she bought a typewriter at a garage sale to put her words into print, and in sixth grade she added illustrations. Now that she has decided what she wants to be when she grows up, A.M. writes books for girls and boys full time. She was selected as the Writer of the Year in 2019-2020 by the League of Utah Writers.

A.M. is the mother of a 10-year-old and a 13-year-old who often inspire her stories. She lives with her husband and children in northern Utah. She is a devout cat person and avid reader.

A.M. Luzzader's books are appropriate for ages 5-12. Her chapter books are intended for kindergarten to third grade, and her middle grade books are for third grade through sixth grade. Find out more about A.M., sign up to receive her newsletter, and get special offers at her website: www.amluzzader.com.

facebook.com/a.m.luzzader

amazon.com/author/amluzzader

ABOUT THE ILLUSTRATOR

Anna Hilton is sixteen years old and has lived in Utah all of her life. She enjoys art, dancing, and spending time with her friends. Anna loves to read novels and to draw pictures of everything she sees.